DOVER
CHILDREN'S THRIFT CLASSICS

The Little Mermaid
and
Other Fairy Tales

HANS CHRISTIAN ANDERSEN

Illustrated by Thea Kliros

DOVER PUBLICATIONS, INC.
New York

DOVER CHILDREN'S THRIFT CLASSICS
EDITOR: PHILIP SMITH

This Dover edition, first published in 1993, contains a new selection of four works (slightly corrected) from *Andersen's Fairy Tales*, edited by Margherita O. Osborne, first published by The Penn Publishing Company, Philadelphia, in 1930. Six illustrations by Thea Kliros and an introductory Note have been specially prepared for this edition.

Library of Congress Cataloging-in-Publication Data

Andersen, H. C. (Hans Christian), 1805–1875.
  The little mermaid and other fairy tales / Hans Christian Andersen ; illustrated by Thea Kliros.
      p.   cm. — (Dover children's thrift classics)
  Summary: Presents "The Little Mermaid," "The Tinder Box," "Great Claus and Little Claus," and "The Swineherd."
  ISBN 0-486-27816-6 (paper)
  1. Fairy tales—Denmark. 2. Children's stories, Danish—Translations into English. [1. Fairy tales. 2. Short stories.] I. Kliros, Thea, ill. II. Title. III. Series.
PZ8.A542Lit   1993c
[Fic]—dc20   93–14418
                                                                          CIP
                                                                          AC

Manufactured in the United States of America
Dover Publications, Inc., 31 East 2nd Street, Mineola, N.Y. 11501

Note

More than any other individual, Danish writer Hans Christian Andersen (1805–1875) is responsible for the creation of the modern children's story. Working out of diverse traditions such as folk tales and the didactic juvenile tracts of his era, Andersen fashioned a distinctive literary type of fairy tale which earned him tremendous popularity during his lifetime and which continues to please readers old and young. This volume contains four of Andersen's most enduring works, which display his skill at blending traditional and original material into entertaining and memorable tales.

Contents

List of Illustrations

The Little Mermaid

FAR OUT AT SEA the water is as blue as the bluest cornflower, and as clear as the clearest crystal, but it is very deep, and if many steeples were piled on the top of one another they would not reach from the bed of the sea to the surface of the water. It is down there that the Mermen live.

The most wonderful trees and plants grow there, and such flexible stalks and leaves, that at the slightest motion of the water they move as if they were alive. All the fish, big and little, glide among the branches just as, up here, birds glide through the air. The palace of the Merman King lies in the very deepest part; its walls are of coral and the long pointed windows of clearest amber, but the roof is made of mussel shells which open and shut with the lapping of the water.

The Merman King had been for many years a widower, but his old mother kept house for

1

him; she was a clever woman, but so proud of her noble birth that she wore twelve oysters on her tail, while the other grandees were only allowed six. Otherwise she was worthy of all praise, especially because she was so fond of the little mermaid princesses, her grandchildren. They were six beautiful children, but the youngest was the prettiest of all, her skin was as soft and delicate as a roseleaf, her eyes as blue as the deepest sea, but like all the others she had no feet, and instead of legs she had a fish's tail.

All the livelong day they used to play in the palace in the great halls, where living flowers grew out of the walls. When the great amber windows were thrown open the fish swam in, just as the swallows fly into our rooms when we open the windows, but the fish swam right up to the little princesses, ate out of their hands, and allowed themselves to be patted.

Outside the palace was a large garden, with fiery red and deep blue trees, the fruit of which shone like gold, while the flowers glowed like fire on their ceaselessly waving stalks. The ground was of the finest sand, but it was of a blue phosphorescent tint. There was a wondrous blue light down there; you might suppose yourself high up in the air, with only the sky above and below you. In a dead calm you could just catch a glimpse of the sun like a purple flower with a stream of light radiating from its calyx.

Each little princess had her own little plot of garden, where she could dig and plant whatever she liked. One made her flower-bed in the shape of a whale, another thought it nice to have hers like a little mermaid; but the youngest made hers quite round like the sun, and she would only have flowers of a rosy hue like its beams. She was a curious child, quiet and thoughtful, and while the other sisters decked out their gardens with all kinds of extraordinary objects which they got from wrecks, she would have nothing but the rosy flowers like the sun up above, except a statue of a beautiful boy. It was hewn out of the purest white marble and had gone to the bottom from some wreck.

Nothing gave her greater pleasure than to hear about the world of human beings up above; she made her old grandmother tell her all that she knew about ships and towns, people and animals. But above all it seemed strangely beautiful to her that up on the earth the flowers were scented, and that the woods were green, and that the fish which were to be seen among the branches could sing so loudly and sweetly that it was a delight to listen

She would have nothing but the rosy flowers
like the sun up above, except a statue of a
beautiful boy.

to them. You see, the grandmother called little birds fish, or the mermaids would not have understood her, as they had never seen a bird.

"When you are fifteen," said the grandmother, "you will be allowed to rise up from the sea and sit on the rocks in the moonlight, and look at the big ships sailing by, and you will also see woods and towns."

One of the sisters would be fifteen in the following year, but the others,—well, they were each one year younger than the other, so that the youngest had five whole years to wait before she would be allowed to come up from the bottom, to see what things were like on earth. But each one promised the others to give a full account of all that she had seen, and found most wonderful on the first day. Their grandmother could never tell them enough, for there were so many things about which they wanted information.

None of them was so full of longings as the youngest, the very one who had the longest time to wait, and who was so quiet and dreamy. Many a night she stood by the open windows and looked up through the dark blue water which the fish were lashing with their tails and fins. She could see the moon and the stars; it is true, their light was pale but they looked much bigger through the water than

they do to our eyes. When she saw a dark
shadow glide between her and them, she
knew that it was either a whale swimming
above her, or else a ship laden with human
beings. I am certain they never dreamed that a
lovely little mermaid was standing down
below, stretching up her white hands towards
the keel.

The eldest princess had now reached her
fifteenth birthday, and was to venture above
the water. When she came back she had hundreds of things to tell them, but the most
delightful of all, she said, was to lie in the
moonlight on a sandbank in a calm sea, and to
gaze at the large town close to the shore,
where the lights twinkled like hundreds of
stars; to listen to music and the noise and bustle of carriages and people, to see the many
church towers and spires, and to hear the
bells ringing; and just because she could not
go on shore she longed for that most of all.

Oh! how eagerly the youngest sister lis-
tened, and when later in the evening she
stood at the open window and looked up
through the dark blue water, she thought of
the big town with all its noise and bustle, and
fancied that she could even hear the church
bells ringing.

The year after, the second sister was

allowed to mount up through the water and swim about wherever she liked. The sun was just going down when she reached the surface, the most beautiful sight, she thought, that she had ever seen. The whole sky had looked like gold, she said, and as for the clouds! well, their beauty was beyond description, they floated in red and violet splendor over her head, and, far faster than they went, a flock of wild swans flew like a long white veil over the water towards the setting sun; she swam towards it, but it sank and all the rosy light on the clouds and water faded away.

The year after that the third sister went up, and being much the most venturesome of them all, swam up a broad river which ran into the sea. She saw beautiful green, vine-clad hills; palaces and country seats peeping through splendid woods. She heard the birds singing, and the sun was so hot that she was often obliged to dive to cool her burning face. In a tiny bay she found a troop of little children running about naked and paddling in the water; she wanted to play with them, but they were frightened and ran away. Then a little black animal came up, it was a dog, but she had never seen one before; it barked so furiously at her that she was frightened and made for the open sea. She could never forget the beautiful woods, the green hills and the lovely children who could swim in the water although they had no fishes' tails.

The fourth sister was not so brave, she stayed in the remotest part of the ocean, and, according to her account, that was the most beautiful spot. You could see for miles and miles around you, and the sky above was like a great glass dome. She had seen ships, but only far away, so that they looked like sea-gulls. There were grotesque dolphins turning somersaults, and gigantic whales squirting water through their nostrils like hundreds of fountains on every side.

Now the fifth sister's turn came. Her birthday fell in the winter, so that she saw sights that the others had not seen on their first trips. The sea looked quite green, and large icebergs were floating about, each one of which looked like a pearl, she said, but was much bigger than the church towers built by men. They took the most wonderful shapes, and sparkled like diamonds. She had seated herself on one of the largest, and all the passing ships sheered off in alarm when they saw her sitting there with her long hair streaming loose in the wind.

In the evening the sky became overcast

with dark clouds; it thundered and lightened, and the huge icebergs, glittering in the bright lightning, were lifted high into the air by the black waves. All the ships shortened sail, and there was fear and trembling on every side, but she sat quietly on her floating iceberg watching the blue lightning flash in zigzags down on to the shining sea.

The first time any of the sisters rose above the water she was delighted by the novelties and beauties she saw; but once grown up, and at liberty to go where she liked, she became indifferent and longed for her home; in the course of a month or so they all said that after all their own home in the deep was best, it was so cozy there.

Many an evening the five sisters interlacing their arms would rise above the water together. They had lovely voices, much clearer than any mortal, and when a storm was rising, and they expected ships to be wrecked, they would sing in the most seductive strains of the wonders of the deep, bidding the seafarers have no fear of them. But the sailors could not understand the words, they thought it was the voice of the storm; nor could it be theirs to see this Elysium of the deep, for when the ship sank they were drowned, and only reached the Merman's palace in death. When the elder sisters rose up in this manner, arm-in-arm, in the evening, the youngest remained behind quite alone, looking after them as if she must weep, but mermaids have no tears and so they suffer all the more.

"Oh! if I were only fifteen!" she said, "I know how fond I shall be of the world above, and of the mortals who dwell there."

At last her fifteenth birthday came.

"Now we shall have you off our hands," said her grandmother, the old queen dowager. "Come now, let me adorn you like your other sisters!" and she put a wreath of white lilies round her hair, but every petal of the flowers was half a pearl; then the old queen had eight oysters fixed on to the princess's tail to show her high rank.

"But it hurts so!" said the little mermaid.

"You must endure the pain for the sake of the finery!" said her grandmother.

But oh! how gladly would she have shaken off all this splendor, and laid aside the heavy wreath. Her red flowers in her garden suited her much better, but she did not dare to make any alteration. "Good-by," she said, and mounted as lightly and airily as a bubble through the water.

The sun had just set when her head rose

above the water, but the clouds were still
lighted up with a rosy and golden splendor,
and the evening star sparkled in the soft pink
sky, the air was mild and fresh, and the sea as
calm as a millpond. A big three-masted ship
lay close by with only a single sail set, for
there was not a breath of wind, and the sailors were sitting about the rigging, on the
crosstrees, and at the mastheads. There was
music and singing on board, and as the
evening closed in, hundreds of gaily colored
lanterns were lighted—they looked like the
flags of all nations waving in the air. The little
mermaid swam right up to the cabin windows,
and every time she was lifted by the swell she
could see through the transparent panes
crowds of gaily dressed people. The handsom-
est of them all was a young prince with large
dark eyes; he could not be much more than
sixteen, and all these festivities were in honor
of his birthday. The sailors danced on deck,
and when the prince appeared among them
hundreds of rockets were let off making it as
light as day, and frightening the little mermaid
so much that she had to dive under the water.
She soon ventured up again, and it was just
as if all the stars of heaven were falling in
showers round about her. She had never seen
such magic fires. Great suns whirled round,

gorgeous fire-fish hung in the blue air, and all was reflected in the calm and glassy sea. It was so light on board the ship that every little rope could be seen, and the people still better. Oh! how handsome the prince was, how he laughed and smiled as he greeted his guests, while the music rang out in the quiet night.

It got quite late, but the little mermaid could not take her eyes off the ship and the beautiful prince. The colored lanterns were put out, no more rockets were sent up, and the cannon had ceased its thunder, but deep down in the sea there was a dull murmuring and moaning sound. Meanwhile she was rocked up and down on the waves, so that she could look into the cabin; but the ship got more and more way on, sail after sail was filled by the wind, the waves grew stronger, great clouds gathered, and it lightened in the distance. Oh, there was going to be a fearful storm! and soon the sailors had to shorten sail. The great ship rocked and rolled as she dashed over the angry sea, the black waves rose like mountains, high enough to overwhelm her, but she dived like a swan through them and rose again and again on their towering crests. The little mermaid thought it a most amusing race, but not so the sailors. The ship creaked and groaned, the mighty timbers bulged and bent under the heavy blows, the water broke over the decks, snapping the mainmast like a reed; she heeled over on her side and the water rushed into the hold.

Now the little mermaid saw that they were in danger and she had for her own sake to beware of the floating beams and wreckage. One moment it was so pitch dark that she could not see at all, but when the lightning flashed it became so light that she could see all on board. Every man was looking out for his own safety as best he could, but she more particularly followed the young prince with her eyes, and when the ship went down she saw him sink in the deep sea. At first she was quite delighted, for now he was coming to be with her, but then she remembered that human beings could not live under water, and that only if he were dead could he go to her father's palace. No! he must not die; so she swam towards him all among the drifting beams and planks, quite forgetting that they might crush her. She dived deep down under the water, and came up again through the waves, and at last reached the young prince just as he was becoming unable to swim any further in the stormy sea. His limbs were numbed, his beautiful eyes were closing, and he must have died if the little mermaid had not come to the rescue. She held his head above the water and let the waves drive them whithersoever they would.

By daybreak all the storm was over, of the ship not a trace was to be seen; the sun rose from the water in radiant brilliance and his rosy beams seemed to cast a glow of life into the prince's cheeks, but his eyes remained closed. The mermaid kissed his fair brow, and stroked back the dripping hair; it seemed to her that he was like the marble statue in her little garden, she kissed him again and longed that he might live.

At last she saw dry land before her, high blue mountains on whose summits the white snow glistened as if a flock of swans had settled there; down by the shore were beautiful green woods, and in the foreground a church or temple, she did not quite know which, but it was a building of some sort. Lemon and orange trees grew in the garden and lofty palms stood by the gate. At this point the sea formed a little bay where the water was quite calm, but very deep, right up to the cliffs; at their foot was a strip of fine white sand to which she swam with the beautiful prince, and laid him down on it, taking great care that his head should rest high up in the warm sunshine.

The bells now began to ring in the great white building and a number of young maidens came into the garden. Then the little mermaid swam further off behind some high rocks and covered her hair and breast with foam, so that no one should see her little face, and then she watched to see who would discover the poor prince.

It was not long before one of the maidens came up to him; at first she seemed quite frightened, but only for a moment, and then she fetched several others, and the mermaid saw that the prince was coming to life, and that he smiled at all those around him, but he never smiled at her; you see he did not know that she had saved him; she felt so sad that when he was led away into the great building she dived sorrowfully into the water and made her way home to her father's palace.

Always silent and thoughtful, she became more so now than ever. Her sisters often asked her what she had seen on her first visit to the surface, but she never would tell them anything.

Many an evening and many a morning she would rise to the place where she had left the prince. She saw the fruit in the garden ripen, and then gathered, she saw the snow melt on the mountain-tops, but she never saw the prince, so she always went home still sadder than before. At home her only consolation was to sit in her little garden with her arms twined round the handsome marble statue which reminded her of the prince. It was all in gloomy shade now, as she had ceased to tend her flowers and the garden had become a neglected wilderness of long stalks and leaves entangled with the branches of the tree.

At last she could not bear it any longer, so she told one of her sisters, and from her it soon spread to the others, but to no one else except to one or two other mermaids who only told their dearest friends. One of these knew all about the prince, she had also seen the festivities on the ship; she knew where he came from and where his kingdom was situated.

"Come, little sister!" said the other princesses, and, throwing their arms round each other's shoulders, they rose from the water in a long line, just in front of the prince's palace.

It was built of light yellow glistening stone, with great marble staircases, one of which led into the garden. Magnificent gilded cupolas rose above the roof, and the spaces between the columns which encircled the building were filled with lifelike marble statues. Through the clear glass of the lofty windows you could see gorgeous halls adorned with costly silken hangings, and the pictures on the walls were a sight worth seeing. In the midst of the central hall a large fountain played, throwing its jets of spray upwards to a glass dome in the roof, through which the sunbeams lighted up the water and the beautiful plants which grew in the great basin.

She knew now where he lived and often used to go there in the evenings and by night over the water; she swam much nearer the land than any of the others dared, she even ventured right up the narrow channel under the splendid marble terrace which threw a long shadow over the water. She used to sit here looking at the young prince who thought he was quite alone in the clear moonlight.

She saw him many an evening sailing about in his beautiful boat, with flags waving and music playing, she used to peep through the green rushes, and if the wind happened to catch her long silvery veil and anyone saw it, they only thought it was a swan flapping its wings.

Many a night she heard the fishermen, who were fishing by torchlight, talking over the good deeds of the young prince; and she was happy to think that she had saved his life when he was drifting about on the waves, half dead, and she could not forget how closely his head had pressed her breast, and how passionately she had kissed him; but he knew nothing of all this, and never saw her even in his dreams.

She became fonder and fonder of mankind, and longed more and more to be able to live among them; their world seemed so infinitely bigger than hers; with their ships they could scour the ocean, they could ascend the mountains high above the clouds, and their wooded, grass-grown lands extended further than her eye could reach. There was so much that she wanted to know, but her sisters could not give an answer to all her questions, so she asked her old grandmother who knew the upper world well, and rightly called it the country above the sea.

"If men are not drowned," asked the little mermaid, "do they live forever, do they not die as we do down here in the sea?"

"Yes," said the old lady, "they have to die too, and their lifetime is even shorter than ours. We may live here for three hundred years, but when we cease to exist, we become mere foam on the water and do not have so much as a grave among our dear ones. We have no immortal souls, we have no future life, we are just like the green seaweed, which, once cut down, can never revive again! Men, on the other hand, have a soul which lives forever, lives after the body has become dust; it rises through the clear air, up to the shining stars! Just as we rise from the water to see the land of mortals, so they rise up to unknown beautiful regions which we shall never see."

"Why have we no immortal souls?" asked the little mermaid sadly. "I would give all my three hundred years to be a human being for one day, and afterwards to have a share in the heavenly kingdom."

"You must not be thinking about that," said the grandmother; "we are much better off and happier than human beings."

"Then I shall have to die and to float as foam on the water, and never hear the music of the waves or see the beautiful flowers or the red sun! Is there nothing I can do to gain an immortal soul?"

"No," said the grandmother, "only if a human being so loved you, that you were more to him than father or mother, if all his thoughts and all his love were so centered in you that he would let the priest join your hands and would vow to be faithful to you here, and to all eternity; then your body would become infused with his soul. Thus and only thus, could you gain a share in the felicity of mankind. He would give you a soul while yet keeping his own. But that can never happen! That which is your greatest beauty in the sea, your fish's tail, is thought hideous up on earth, so little do they understand about it; to be pretty there you must have two clumsy supports which they call legs!"

Then the little mermaid sighed and looked sadly at her fish's tail.

"Let us be happy," said the grandmother, "we will hop and skip during our three hundred years of life, it is surely a long enough time, and after it is over, we shall rest all the better in our graves. There is to be a court ball to-night."

This was a much more splendid affair than we ever see on earth. The walls and the ceiling of the great ballroom were of thick but transparent glass. Several hundreds of colossal mussel shells, rose-red and grass-green, were ranged in order round the sides holding blue lights, which illuminated the whole room and shone through the walls, so that the sea outside was quite lit up. You could see countless fish, great and small, swimming towards the glass walls, some with shining scales of crimson hue, while others were golden and silvery. In the middle of the room was a broad stream of running water, and on this the mermaids and mermen danced to their own beautiful singing. No earthly beings have such lovely voices. The little mermaid sang more sweetly than any of them and they all applauded her. For a moment she felt glad at heart, for she knew that she had the finest voice either in the sea or on land. But she soon began to think again about the upper world, she could not forget the handsome prince and her sorrow in not possessing, like him, an immortal soul. Therefore she stole out of her father's palace, and while all within was joy and merriment, she sat sadly in her little garden. Suddenly she heard the sound of a horn through the water, and she thought, "Now he is out sailing up there; he whom I love more than father or mother, he to whom my thoughts cling and to whose hands I am ready to commit the happiness of my life. I will dare anything to win him and to gain an immortal soul! While my sisters are dancing in my father's palace, I will go to the sea witch of whom I have always been very much afraid, she will perhaps be able to advise and help me!"

Thereupon the little mermaid left the garden and went towards the roaring whirlpools at the back of which the witch lived. She had

never been that way before; no flowers grew
there, no seaweed, only the bare gray sands,
stretched towards the whirlpools, which like
rushing millwheels swirled round, dragging
everything that came within reach down to
the depths. She had to pass between these
boiling eddies to reach the witch's domain,
and for a long way the only path led over
warm bubbling mud, which the witch called
her "peat bog." Her house stood behind this in
the midst of a weird forest. All the trees and
bushes were polyps, half animal and half
plant; they looked like hundred-headed
snakes growing out of the sand, the branches
were long slimy arms, with tentacles like
wriggling worms, every joint of which from
the root to the outermost tip was in constant
motion. They wound themselves tightly round
whatever they could lay hold of and never let
it escape. The little mermaid standing outside
was quite frightened, her heart beat fast with
terror and she nearly turned back, but then
she remembered the prince and the immortal
soul of mankind and took courage. She bound
her long flowing hair tightly round her head,
so that the polyps should not seize her by it,
folded her hands over her breast, and darted
like a fish through the water, in between the
hideous polyps which stretched out their sen-

she gave such a loud hideous laugh that
oad and snakes fell to the ground and
led about there.

u are just in the nick of time," said the
; "after sunrise to-morrow I should not
le to help you until another year had run
ourse. I will make you a potion, and
e sunrise you must swim ashore with it,
ourself on the beach and drink it; then
tail will divide and shrivel up to what
all beautiful legs, but it hurts, it is as if a
sword were running through you. All
ee you will say that you are the most
ful child of man they have ever seen.
ill keep your gliding gait, no dancer will
ou, but every step you take will be as if
ere treading upon sharp knives, so
as to draw blood. If you are willing to
all this I am ready to help you!"

" said the little princess with a trem-
oice, thinking of the prince and of win-
undying soul.

remember," said the witch, "when once
ave received a human form, you can
be a mermaid again, you will never
e able to dive down through the water
r sisters and to your father's palace.
you do not succeed in winning the
s love, so that for your sake he will for-

sitive arms and tentacl
could see that every on
thing or other, which th
their hundred arms, and
in iron bands. The ble
who had perished at
peeped forth from the
others clutched rudders
skeleton of some land a
ble of all, a little mer
caught and suffocated.
large opening in the w
was all slimy, and whei
snakes were gamboliɲ
of this opening was a h
of the wrecked; there
toad eat out of her moɪ
little canary eat sugar.
water snakes her littlɛ
them to crawl about oɪ

"I know very well w
for," said the witch. "ɪ
All the same you shall
it will lead you into r
cess. You want to ge
and instead to have tv
upon like human be
prince may fall in lov
may win him and aɪ

this,
the t
wrigg
"Yc
witch
be ab
its c
befor
seat y
your
men c
sharp
who s
beauti
You w
rival y
you v
sharp
suffer
"Yes
bling v
ning aɪ
"But
you h.
never
again ɪ
to you
And if
prince'

get father and mother, cleave to you with his whole heart, let the priest join your hands and make you man and wife, you will gain no immortal soul! The first morning after his marriage with another your heart will break, and you will turn into foam of the sea."

"I will do it," said the little mermaid as pale as death.

"But you will have to pay me, too," said the witch, "and it is no trifle that I demand. You have the most beautiful voice of any at the bottom of the sea, and I daresay that you think you will fascinate him with it, but you must give me that voice. I will have the best you possess in return for my precious potion! I have to mingle my own blood with it so as to make it as sharp as a two-edged sword."

"But if you take my voice," said the little mermaid, "what have I left?"

"Your beautiful form," said the witch, "your gliding gait, and your speaking eyes, with these you ought surely to be able to bewitch a human heart. Well! have you lost courage? Put out your little tongue and I will cut it off in payment for the powerful draught."

"Let it be done," said the little mermaid, and the witch put on her cauldron to brew the magic potion. "There is nothing like cleanliness," said she, as she scoured the pot with a bundle of snakes; then she punctured her breast and let the black blood drop into the cauldron, and the steam took the most weird shape, enough to frighten anyone. Every moment the witch threw new ingredients into the pot, and when it boiled the bubbling was like the sound of crocodiles weeping. At last the potion was ready and it looked like the clearest water.

"There it is," said the witch, and thereupon she cut off the tongue of the little mermaid, who was dumb now and could neither sing nor speak.

"If the polyps should seize you, when you go back through my wood," said the witch, "just drop a single drop of this liquid on them, and their arms and fingers will burst into a thousand pieces." But the little mermaid had no need to do this, for at the mere sight of the bright liquid which sparkled in her hand like a shining star, they drew back in terror. So she soon got past the wood, the bog, and the eddying whirlpools.

She saw her father's palace, the lights were all out in the great ballroom, and no doubt all the household was asleep, but she did not dare to go in now that she was dumb and about to leave her home forever. She felt as if her heart would break with grief. She stole into the garden and plucked a flower from each of her sister's plots, wafted with her hand countless kisses towards the palace, and then rose up through the dark blue water.

The sun had not risen when she came in sight of the prince's palace and landed at the beautiful marble steps. The moon was shining bright and clear. The little mermaid drank the burning, stinging draught, and it was like a sharp, two-edged sword running through her tender frame; she fainted away and lay as if she were dead. When the sun rose on the sea she woke up and became conscious of a sharp pang, but just in front of her stood the handsome young prince, fixing his coal black eyes on her; she saw that her fish's tail was gone, and that she had the prettiest little white legs any maiden could desire, but she was quite naked, so she wrapped her long thick hair around her. The prince asked who she was and how she came there; she looked at him tenderly and with a sad expression in her dark blue eyes, but could not speak. Then he took her by the hand and led her into the palace. Every step she took was, as the witch had warned her beforehand, as if she were treading on sharp knives and spikes but she bore it gladly; led by the prince she moved as lightly as a bubble, and he and everyone else marveled at her graceful gliding gait.

Clothed in the costliest silks and muslins

she was the greatest beauty in the palace, but she was dumb and could neither sing nor speak. Beautiful slaves clad in silks and gold came forward and sang to the prince and his royal parents; one of them sang better than all the others, and the prince clapped his hands and smiled at her; that made the little mermaid very sad, for she knew that she used to sing far better herself. She thought, "Oh! if he only knew that for the sake of being with him I had given up my voice forever!" Now the slaves began to dance, graceful undulating dances to enchanting music; thereupon the little mermaid lifting her beautiful white arms and raising herself on tiptoe glided on the floor with a grace which none of the other dancers had yet attained. With every motion her grace and beauty became more apparent, and her eyes appealed more deeply to the heart than the songs of the slaves. Everyone was delighted with it, especially the prince, who called her his foundling, and she danced on and on, notwithstanding that every time her foot touched the ground it was like treading on sharp knives. The prince said that she should always be near him, and she was allowed to sleep outside his door on a velvet cushion.

He had a man's dress made for her, so that

With every motion her grace and beauty became
more apparent.

she could ride about with him. They used to ride through scented woods, where the green branches brushed her shoulders, and little birds sang among the fresh leaves. She climbed up the highest mountains with the prince, and although her delicate feet bled so that others saw it, she only laughed and followed him until they saw the clouds sailing below them like a flock of birds, taking flight to distant lands.

At home in the prince's palace, when at night the others were asleep, she used to go out on to the marble steps; it cooled her burning feet to stand in the cold sea water, and at such times she used to think of those she had left in the deep.

One night her sisters came arm in arm; they sang so sorrowfully as they swam on the water that she beckoned to them and they recognized her, and told her how she had grieved them all. After that they visited her every night, and one night she saw, a long way out, her old grandmother (who for many years had not been above the water), and the Merman King with his crown on his head; they stretched out their hands towards her, but did not venture so close to land as her sisters.

Day by day she became dearer to the prince, he loved her as one loves a good sweet child, but it never entered his head to make her his queen; yet unless she became his wife she would never win an everlasting soul, but on his wedding morning would turn to sea foam.

"Am I not dearer to you than any of them?" the little mermaid's eyes seemed to say when he took her in his arms and kissed her beautiful brow.

"Yes, you are the dearest one to me," said the prince, "for you have the best heart of them all, and you are fondest of me; you are also like a young girl I once saw, but whom I never expect to see again. I was on board a ship which was wrecked, I was driven on shore by the waves close to a holy Temple where several young girls were ministering at a service; the youngest of them found me on the beach and saved my life; I saw her but twice. She was the only person I could love in this world, but you are like her, you almost drive her image out of my heart. She belongs to the holy Temple, and therefore by good fortune you have been sent to me, we will never part!"

"Alas! he does not know that it was I who saved his life," thought the little mermaid. "I bore him over the sea to the wood, where the Temple stands. I sat behind the foam and watched to see if anyone would come. I saw the pretty girl he loves better than me." And the mermaid heaved a bitter sigh, for she could not weep.

"The girl belongs to the holy Temple, he has said, she will never return to the world, they will never meet again, I am here with him, I see him every day. Yes! I will tend him, love him, and give up my life to him."

But now the rumor ran that the prince was to be married to the beautiful daughter of a neighboring king, and for that reason was fitting out a splendid ship. It was given out that the prince was going on a voyage to see the adjoining countries, but it was without doubt to see the king's daughter; he was to have a great suite with him, but the little mermaid shook her head and laughed; she knew the prince's intentions much better than any of the others. "I must take this voyage," he had said to her; "I must go and see the beautiful princess; my parents demand that, but they will never force me to bring her home as my bride; I can never love her! She will not be like the lovely girl in the Temple whom you resemble. If ever I had to choose a bride it would sooner be you with your speaking eyes, my sweet, dumb foundling!" And he kissed her rosy mouth, played with her long hair, and laid his head upon her heart, which already dreamed of human joys and an immortal soul.

"You are not frightened of the sea, I suppose, my dumb child?" he said, as they stood on the proud ship which was to carry them to the country of the neighboring king; and he told her about storms and calms, about curious fish in the deep, and the marvels seen by divers; and she smiled at his tales, for she knew all about the bottom of the sea much better than anyone else.

At night, in the moonlight, when all were asleep, except the steersman who stood at the helm, she sat at the side of the ship trying to pierce the clear water with her eyes, and fancied she saw her father's palace, and above it her old grandmother with her silver crown on her head, looking up through the cross currents towards the keel of the ship. Then her sisters rose above the water, they gazed sadly at her, wringing their white hands; she beckoned to them, smiled, and was about to tell them that all was going well and happily with her, when the cabin boy approached, and the sisters dived down, but he supposed that the white objects he had seen were nothing but flakes of foam.

The next morning the ship entered the harbor of the neighboring king's magnificent city.

The church bells rang and trumpets were sounded from every lofty tower, while the soldiers paraded with flags flying and glittering bayonets. There was a fête every day, there was a succession of balls, and receptions followed one after the other, but the princess was not yet present, she was being brought up a long way off, in a holy Temple they said, and was learning all the royal virtues. At last she came. The little mermaid stood eager to see her beauty, she was obliged to confess that a lovelier creature she had never beheld. Her complexion was exquisitely pure and delicate, and her trustful eyes of the deepest blue shone through their dark lashes.

"It is you," said the prince, "you who saved me when I lay almost lifeless on the beach?" and he clasped his blushing bride to his heart. "Oh! I am too happy!" he exclaimed to the little mermaid.

"A greater joy than I had dared to hope for has come to pass. You will rejoice at my joy, for you love me better than anyone." Then the little mermaid kissed his hand, and felt as if her heart were broken already.

His wedding morn would bring death to her and change her to foam.

All the church bells pealed and heralds rode through the town proclaiming the nuptials.

Upon every altar throughout the land fragrant oil was burned in costly silver lamps. Amidst the swinging of censers by the priests, the bride and bridegroom joined hands and received the bishop's blessing. The little mermaid dressed in silk and gold stood holding the bride's train, but her ears were deaf to the festal strains, her eyes saw nothing of the sacred ceremony, she was thinking of her coming death and of all that she had lost in this world.

That same evening the bride and bridegroom embarked, amidst the roar of cannon and the waving of banners. A royal tent of purple and gold softly cushioned was raised amidships where the bridal pair were to repose during the cool night.

The sails swelled in the wind and the ship skimmed lightly and almost without motion over the transparent sea.

At dusk lanterns of many colors were lighted and the sailors danced merrily on deck. The little mermaid could not help thinking of the first time she came up from the sea and saw the same splendor and gayety; and she now threw herself among the dancers, whirling, as a swallow skims through the air when pursued. The onlookers cheered her in amazement, never had she danced so divinely;

her delicate feet pained her as if they were cut with knives, but she did not feel it, for the pain at her heart was much sharper. She knew that it was the last night that she would breathe the same air as he, and would look upon the mighty deep, and the blue starry heavens; an endless night without thought and without dreams awaited her, who neither had a soul, nor could win one. The joy and revelry on board lasted till long past midnight, she went on laughing and dancing with the thought of death all the time in her heart. The prince caressed his lovely bride and she played with his raven locks, and with their arms entwined they retired to the gorgeous tent. All became hushed and still on board the ship, only the steersman stood at the helm, the little mermaid laid her white arms on the gunwale and looked eastwards for the pink tinted dawn; the first sunbeam, she knew, would be her death. Then she saw her sisters rise from the water, they were as pale as she was, their beautiful long hair no longer floated on the breeze, for it had been cut off.

"We have given it to the witch to obtain her help, so that you may not die to-night! she has given us a knife, here it is, look how sharp it is! Before the sun rises, you must plunge it into the prince's heart, and when his warm blood sprinkles your feet they will join together and grow into a tail, and you will once more be a mermaid; you will be able to come down into the water to us, and to live out your three hundred years before you are turned into dead, salt, sea-foam. Make haste! you or he must die before sunrise! Our old grandmother is so full of grief that her white hair has fallen off as ours fell under the witch's scissors. Slay the prince and come back to us! Quick! Quick! do you not see the rosy streak in the sky? In a few moments the sun will rise and then you must die!" Saying this they heaved a wondrous deep sigh and sank among the waves.

The little mermaid drew aside the purple curtain from the tent and looked at the beautiful bride asleep with her head on the prince's breast; she bent over him and kissed his fair brow, looked at the sky where the dawn was spreading fast; looked at the sharp knife, and again fixed her eyes on the prince who, in his dream called his bride by name, yes she alone was in his thoughts!—For a moment the knife quivered in her grasp, then she threw it far out among the waves now rosy in the morning light and where it fell the water bubbled up like drops of blood.

Once more she looked at the prince, with

her eyes already dimmed by death, then dashed overboard and fell, her body dissolving into foam.

Now the sun rose from the sea and with its kindly beams warmed the deadly cold foam, so that the little mermaid did not feel the chill of death. She saw the bright sun and above her floated hundreds of beauteous ethereal beings through which she could see the white ship and the rosy heavens, their voices were melodious but so spirit-like that no human ear could hear them, any more than an earthly eye could see their forms. Light as bubbles they floated through the air without the aid of wings. The little mermaid perceived that she had a form like theirs, it gradually took shape out of the foam. "To whom am I coming?" said she, and her voice sounded like that of the other beings, so unearthly in its beauty that no music of ours could reproduce it.

"To the daughters of the air!" answered the others; "a mermaid has no undying soul, and can never gain one without winning the love of a human being. Her eternal life must depend upon an unknown power. Nor have the daughters of the air an everlasting soul, but by their own good deeds they may create one for themselves. We fly to the tropics where mankind is the victim of hot and pestilent winds, there we bring cooling breezes. We diffuse the scent of flowers all around, and bring refreshment and healing in our train. When, for three hundred years, we have labored to do all the good in our power we gain an undying soul and take a part in the everlasting joys of mankind. You, poor little mermaid, have with your whole heart, struggled for the same thing as we have struggled for. You have suffered and endured, raised yourself to the spirit world of the air; and now, by your own good deeds you may, in the course of three hundred years, work out for yourself an undying soul."

Then the little mermaid lifted her transparent arms towards God's sun, and for the first time shed tears.

On board ship all was again life and bustle, she saw the prince with his lovely bride searching for her, they looked sadly at the bubbling foam, as if they knew that she had thrown herself into the waves. Unseen she kissed the bride on her brow, smiled at the prince and rose aloft with the other spirits of the air to the rosy clouds which sailed above.

"In three hundred years we shall thus float into Paradise."

"We might reach it sooner," whispered one. "Unseen we flit into those homes of men

where there are children, and for every day
that we find a good child who gives pleasure
to its parents and deserves their love, God
shortens our time of probation. The child
does not know when we fly through the room,
and when we smile with pleasure at it, one
year of our three hundred is taken away.
But if we see a naughty or badly disposed
child, we cannot help shedding tears of sorrow, and every tear adds a day to the time of
our probation."

The Tinder Box

A SOLDIER CAME marching along the highroad. One, two! One, two! He had his knapsack on his back and his sword at his side, for he had been to the wars and he was on his way home now. He met an old witch on the road. She was so ugly, her lower lip hung right down on to her chin.

She said, "Good-evening, soldier! What a nice sword you've got, and such a big knapsack; you are a real soldier! You shall have as much money as ever you like!"

"Thank you kindly, you old witch!" said the soldier.

"Do you see that big tree!" said the witch, pointing to a tree close by. "It is hollow inside! Climb up to the top and you will see a hole into which you can let yourself down, right down under the tree! I will tie a rope round your waist so that I can haul you up again when you call!"

"What am I to do down under that tree?" asked the soldier.

"Fetch money!" said the witch. "You must know that when you get down to the bottom of the tree you will find yourself in a wide passage; it's quite light there, for there are over a hundred blazing lamps. You will see three doors which you can open, for the keys are there. If you go into the first room you will see a big box in the middle of the floor. A dog is sitting on top of it, and he has eyes as big as saucers, but you needn't mind that. I will give you my blue checked apron, which you can spread out on the floor; then go quickly forward, take up the dog and put him on my apron, open the box and take out as much money as ever you like. It is all copper, but if you like silver better, go into the next room. There you will find a dog with eyes as big as millstones; but never mind that, put him on my apron and take the money. If you prefer gold you can have it too, and as much as you can carry, if you go into the third room. But the dog sitting on that box has eyes each as big as the Round Tower. He is a dog, indeed, as you may imagine! But don't let it trouble you; you only have to put him on to my apron and then he won't hurt you, and you can take as much gold out of the box as you like!"

"That's not so bad!" said the soldier. "But what am I to give you, old witch? For you'll want something, I'll be bound."

"No," said the witch, "not a single penny do I want. I only want you to bring me an old tinder box that my grandmother forgot the last time she was down there!"

"Well! tie the rope round my waist!" said the soldier.

"Here it is," said the witch, "and here is my blue-checked apron."

Then the soldier climbed up the tree, let himself slide down the hollow trunk, and found himself, as the witch had said, in the wide passage where the many hundred lamps were burning.

Now he opened the first door. Ugh! There sat the dog with eyes as big as saucers, staring at him.

"You are a nice fellow!" said the soldier, as he put him on to the witch's apron, and took out as many pennies as he could cram into his pockets. Then he shut the box, and put the dog on top of it again, and went into the next room. Hallo! there sat the dog with eyes as big as millstones.

"You shouldn't stare at me so hard! You might get a pain in your eyes!" Then he put

Then the soldier climbed up the tree.

the dog on the apron, but when he saw all the silver in the box he threw away all the coppers and stuffed his pockets and his knapsack with silver. Then he went on into the third room. Oh! how horrible! that dog really had two big eyes as big as the Round Tower, and they rolled round and round like wheels.

"Good-evening!" said the soldier, saluting, for he had never seen such a dog in his life; but after looking at him for a bit he thought, "That will do," and he lifted him down on to the apron and opened the chest. Preserve us! What a lot of gold! He could buy the whole of Copenhagen with it, and all the sugar pigs from the cake-women, all the tin soldiers, whips and rocking-horses in the world! That was money indeed! Now the soldier threw away all the silver he had filled his pockets and his knapsack with, and put gold in its place. Yes, he crammed all his pockets, his knapsack, his cap and his boots so full that he could hardly walk! Now, he really had got a lot of money. He put the dog back on to the box, shut the door, and shouted up through the tree, "Haul me up, you old witch!"

"Have you got the tinder box?"

"Oh! to be sure!" said the soldier. "I had quite forgotten it." And he went back to fetch it. The witch hauled him up, and there he was, standing on the highroad again with his pockets, boots, knapsack and cap full of gold.

"What do you want the tinder box for?" asked the soldier.

"That's no business of yours," said the witch. "You've got the money. Give me the tinder box!"

"Rubbish!" said the soldier. "Tell me directly what you want with it, or I will draw my sword and cut off your head."

"I won't!" said the witch.

Then the soldier cut off her head. There she lay, but he tied all the money up in her apron, slung it on his back like a pack, put the tinder box in his pocket, and marched off to the town.

It was a beautiful town, and he went straight to the finest hotel, ordered the grandest rooms and all the food he liked best, for he was a rich man, now that he had so much money.

Certainly the servant who had to clean his boots thought they were very funny old things for such a rich gentleman, but he had not had time yet to buy any new ones; the next day he bought new boots and fine clothes. The soldier now became a fine gentleman, and the people told him all about the grand things in the town, and about their king, and what a lovely princess his daughter was.

"Where is she to be seen?" asked the soldier.

"You can't see her at all!" they all said. "She lives in a great copper castle surrounded with walls and towers. Nobody but the king dare go in and out, for it has been prophesied that she will marry a common soldier, and the king doesn't like that!"

"I should like to see her well enough!" thought the soldier. But there was no way of getting leave for that.

He now led a very merry life, went to theaters, drove about in the King's Park, and gave away a lot of money to the poor people, which was very nice of him; for he remembered how disagreeable it used to be not to have a penny in his pocket. Now he was rich, wore fine clothes, and had a great many friends, who all said what a nice fellow he was—a thorough gentleman—and he liked to be told that.

But as he went on spending money every day and his store was never renewed, he at last found himself with only two pence left. Then he was obliged to move out of his fine rooms. He had to take a tiny little attic up under the roof, clean his own boots, and mend them, himself, with a darning needle.

None of his friends went to see him, because there were far too many stairs.

One dark evening, when he had not even enough money to buy a candle with, he suddenly remembered that there was a little bit in the old tinder box he had brought out of the hollow tree, when the witch helped him down. He got out the tinder box with the candle end in it and struck fire. As the sparks flew out from the flint, the door burst open and the dog with eyes as big as saucers, which he had seen down under the tree, stood before him and said, "What does my lord command?"

"By heaven!" said the soldier, "this is a nice kind of tinder box, if I can get whatever I want like this! Get me some money," he said to the dog, and away it went.

It was back in a twinkling with a big bag full of pennies in its mouth.

Now the soldier saw what a treasure he had in the tinder box. If he struck once, the dog which sat on the box of copper came; if he struck twice, the dog on the silver box came; and if he struck three times, the one from the box of gold.

He now moved down to the grand rooms and got his fine clothes again, and then all his friends knew him once more and liked him as much as ever.

Then he began to think: After all, it's a curious thing that no man can get a sight of the princess! Everyone says she is so beautiful! But what is the good of that, when she always has to be shut up in that big copper palace with all the towers. Can I not somehow manage to see her? Where is my tinder box? Then he struck the flint, and, whisk, came the dog with eyes as big as saucers.

"It certainly is the middle of the night," said the soldier, "but I am very anxious to see the princess, if only for a single moment."

The dog was out of the door in an instant, and before the soldier had time to think about it, he was back again with the princess. There she was, fast asleep on the dog's back, and she was so lovely that anybody could see that she must be a real princess! The soldier could not help it; he was obliged to kiss her, for he was a true soldier.

Then the dog ran back again with the princess, but in the morning when the king and queen were having breakfast, the princess said that she had had such a wonderful dream about a dog and a soldier. She had ridden on the dog's back, and the soldier had kissed her.

"That's a pretty tale," said the queen.

After this an old lady-in-waiting had to sit by her bed at night to see if this was really a dream.

The soldier longed so intensely to see the

princess again that at night the dog came to fetch her. He took her up and ran off with her as fast as he could, but the old lady-in-waiting put on her galoshes and ran just as fast behind them. When she saw that they disappeared into a large house, she thought, now I know where it is, and made a big cross with chalk on the gate. Then she went home and lay down, and presently the dog came back, too, with the princess. When the dog saw that there was a cross on the gate, he took a bit of chalk, too, and made crosses on all the gates in the town. Now this was very clever of him, for the lady-in-waiting could not possibly find the gate when there were crosses on all the gates.

Early next morning the king, and queen, the lady-in-waiting, and all the court officials went to see where the princess had been.

"There it is," said the king, when he saw the first door with the cross on it.

"No, my dear husband, it is there," said the queen, who saw another door with a cross on it.

"But there is one, and there is another!" they all cried out.

They soon saw that it was hopeless to try and find it.

Now the queen was a very clever woman;

she knew more than how to drive in a chariot. She took her big gold scissors and cut up a large piece of silk into small pieces, and made a pretty little bag, which she filled with fine grains of buckwheat. She then tied it on the back of the princess, and when that was done, she cut a little hole in the bag, so that the grains could drop out all the way wherever the princess went.

At night the dog came again, took the princess on his back, and ran off with her to the soldier, who was so fond of her that he longed to be a prince, so that he might have her for his wife.

The dog never noticed how the grain dropped out all along the road from the palace to the soldier's window, where he ran up the wall with the princess.

In the morning the king and queen easily saw where their daughter had been, and they seized the soldier and threw him into the dungeons.

There he lay! Oh, how dark and tiresome it was, and then one day they said to him, "To-morrow you are to be hanged." It was not amusing to be told that, especially as he had left his tinder box behind him at the hotel.

In the morning he could see through the bars in the little window that people were hurrying out of the town to see him hanged. He heard the drums and saw the soldiers go marching along. All the world was going; among them was a shoemaker's boy in his leather apron and slippers. He was in such a hurry that he lost one of his slippers, and it fell close under the soldier's window where he was peeping through the bars. "I say, you boy! Don't be in such a hurry," said the soldier to him. "Nothing will happen till I get there! But if you will run to the house where I used to live, and fetch me my tinder box, you shall have a penny!"

The boy was only too glad to have the penny, and tore off to get the tinder box, gave it to the soldier, and—yes, now we shall hear!

Outside the town a high scaffold had been raised, and the soldiers were drawn up round about it, as well as crowds of townspeople. The king and the queen sat upon a beautiful throne exactly opposite the judge and all the councillors.

The soldier mounted the ladder, but when they were about to put the rope round his neck, he said that, before undergoing his punishment, a criminal was always allowed the gratification of a harmless wish, and he wanted very much to smoke a pipe, as it would be his last pipe in this world.

The king could not deny him this, so the soldier took out his tinder box and struck fire, once, twice, three times, and there were all the dogs. The one with eyes like saucers, the one with eyes like millstones, and the one whose eyes were as big as the Round Tower.

"Help me! Save me from being hanged!" cried the soldier.

And then the dogs rushed at the soldiers and the councillors; they took one by the legs, and another by the nose, and threw them up many fathoms into the air; and when they fell down, they were all broken to pieces.

"I won't!" cried the king, but the biggest dog took both him and the queen and threw them after all the others. Then the soldiers became alarmed, and the people shouted, "Oh! good soldier, you shall be our king and marry the beautiful princess!"

So they conducted the soldier to the king's chariot, and all three dogs danced along in front of him and shouted "Hurrah!" The boys all put their fingers in their mouths and whistled, and the soldiers presented arms. The princess came out of the copper palace and became queen, which pleased her very much. The wedding took place in a week, and the dogs all had seats at the table, where they sat staring with all their eyes.

Great Claus and Little Claus

IN A VILLAGE there once lived two men of the self-same name. They were both called Claus, but one of them had four horses, and the other only had one; so to distinguish them people called the owner of the four horses "Great Claus," and he who had only one "Little Claus." Now I shall tell you what happened to them, for this is a true story.

Throughout the week Little Claus was obliged to plow for Great Claus, and to lend him his one horse; but once a week, on Sunday, Great Claus lent him all his four horses.

"Hurrah!" How Little Claus would smack his whip over all five, for they were as good as his own on that one day.

The sun shone brightly and the church bells rang merrily as the people passed by, dressed in their best, with their prayer-books under their arms. They were going to hear the parson preach. They looked at Little Claus plowing with his five horses, and he was so proud that he smacked his whip and said, "Gee-up, my five horses."

"You mustn't say that," said Great Claus, "for only one of them is yours."

But Little Claus soon forgot what he ought not to say, and when anyone passed, he would call out, "Gee-up, my five horses."

"I must really beg you not to say that again," said Great Claus, "for if you do, I shall hit your horse on the head, so that he will drop down dead on the spot, and there will be an end of him."

"I promise you I will not say it again," said the other; but as soon as anybody came by nodding to him, and wishing him "Good-day," he was so pleased, and thought how grand it was to have five horses plowing in his field, that he cried out again, "Gee-up, all my horses!"

"I'll gee-up your horses for you," said Great Claus, and seizing the tethering mallet he struck Little Claus' one horse on the head, and it fell down dead.

"Oh, now I have no horse at all," said Little Claus, weeping. But after a long while he flayed the dead horse, and hung up the skin in the wind to dry.

Then he put the dry skin into a bag, and hanging it over his shoulder went off to the next town to sell it. But he had a long way to go, and had to pass through a dark and gloomy forest.

Presently a storm arose, and he lost his way; and before he discovered the right path evening was drawing on, and it was still a long way to the town, and too far to return home before nightfall.

Near the road stood a large farmhouse. The shutters outside the windows were closed, but lights shone through the crevices and at the top. "They might let me stay here for the night," thought Little Claus, so he went up to the door and knocked. The farmer's wife opened the door, but when she heard what he wanted, she told him to go away; her husband was not at home, and she could not let any strangers in.

"Then I shall have to lie out here," said Little Claus to himself as the farmer's wife shut the door in his face.

Close to the farmhouse stood a large haystack, and between it and the house there was a small shed with a thatched roof. "I can lie up there," said Little Claus, looking at the roof. "It will make a famous bed, but I hope

the stork won't fly down and bite my legs." A
live stork was standing up there who had his
nest on the roof.

So Little Claus climbed on the roof of the
shed, and as he turned about to make himself
comfortable he discovered that the wooden
shutters did not reach to the top of the windows, so that he could see into the room, in
which a large table was laid out, with wine,
roast meat, and a splendid fish.

The farmer's wife and the sexton were sitting at table together. Nobody else was there.
She was filling his glass and helping him plen-
tifully to fish.

"If only I could have some, too," thought
Little Claus, and then, as he stretched out his
neck towards the window, he spied a beautiful, large cake—indeed they had a glorious
feast before them.

At that moment he heard someone riding
down the road towards the farm. It was the
farmer coming home.

He was a good man, but he had one very
strange prejudice—he could not bear the
sight of a sexton. If he happened to see one,
he would get into a terrible rage. In conse-
quence of this dislike, the sexton had gone to
visit the farmer's wife during her husband's
absence from home, and the good woman had

put before him the best of everything she had
in the house to eat.

When they heard the farmer, they were
dreadfully frightened, and the woman made
the sexton creep into a large chest which
stood in a corner. He went at once, for he was
well aware of the poor man's aversion to the
sight of a sexton. The woman then quickly hid
all the nice things and the wine in the oven,
because if her husband had seen it he would
have asked questions.

"Oh, dear!" sighed Little Claus, on the roof,
when he saw the food disappearing.

"Is there anyone up there?" asked the
farmer, peering up at Little Claus. "What are
you doing up there? You had better come into
the house."

Then Little Claus told him how he had lost
his way, and asked if he might have shelter for
the night.

"Certainly," said the farmer; "but the first
thing is to have something to eat."

The woman received them both very kindly,
laid the table, and gave them a large bowl of
porridge. The farmer was hungry, and ate it
with a good appetite; but Little Claus could
not help thinking of the good roast meat, the
fish and the cake, which he knew were hidden
in the oven.

He put his sack with the hide in it under the table by his feet, for, as we remember, he was on his way to the town to sell it. He did not fancy the porridge, so he trod on the sack and made the dried hide squeak quite loudly.

"Hush!" said Little Claus to his sack, at the same time treading on it again, so that it squeaked louder than ever.

"What on earth have you got in your sack?" asked the farmer again.

"Oh, it's a Goblin," said Little Claus; "he says we needn't eat the porridge, for he has charmed the oven full of roast meat and fish and cake."

"What do you say!" said the farmer, opening the oven door with all speed, and seeing the nice things the woman had hidden, but which her husband thought the Goblin had produced for their special benefit.

The woman dared not say anything, but put the food before them, and then they both made a hearty meal of the fish, the meat and the cake.

Then Little Claus trod on the skin and made it squeak again.

"What does he say now?" asked the farmer.

"He says," answered Little Claus, "that he has also charmed three bottles of wine into the oven for us."

"Hush!" said Little Claus to his sack.

So the woman had to bring out the wine too, and the farmer drank it and became merry. Wouldn't he like to have a Goblin, like the one in Little Claus' sack, for himself?

"Can he charm out the Devil?" asked the farmer. "I shouldn't mind seeing him, now that I am in such a merry mood."

"Oh, yes!" said Little Claus; "my Goblin can do everything that we ask him. Can't you?" he asked, trampling up the sack till it squeaked louder than ever. "Do you hear what I say? But the Devil is so ugly, you'd better not see him."

"Oh! I'm not a bit frightened. Whatever does he look like?"

"Well, he will show himself in the image of a sexton."

"Oh, dear!" said the farmer; "that's bad! I must tell you that I can't bear to see a sexton! However, it doesn't matter! I shall know it's only the Devil, and then I sha'n't mind so much! Now, my courage is up! But he mustn't come too close."

"I'll ask my Goblin about it," said Little Claus, treading on the bag and putting his ear close to it.

"What does he say?"

"He says you can go along and open the chest in the corner, and there you'll see the

Devil moping in the dark; but hold the lid tight so that he doesn't get out."

"Will you help me to hold it?" asked the farmer, going along to the chest where the woman had hidden the real sexton, who was shivering with fright.

The farmer lifted up the lid a wee little bit and peeped in. "Ha!" he shrieked, and sprang back. "Yes, I saw him, and he looked just exactly like our sexton! It was a horrible sight."

They had to have a drink after this, and there they sat drinking till far into the night.

"You must sell me that Goblin," said the farmer. "You may ask what you like for him! I will give you a bushel of money for him."

"No, I can't do that," said Little Claus; "you must remember how useful my Goblin is to me."

"Oh, but I should so like to have him," said the farmer, and he went on begging for him.

"Well," said Little Claus at last, "as you have been so kind to me I shall have to give him up. You shall have my Goblin for a bushel of money, but I must have it full to the brim!"

"You shall have it," said the farmer; "but you must take that chest away with you; I won't have it in the house for another hour."

So Little Claus gave his sack with the dried

hide in it to the farmer, and received in return a bushel of money for it, and the measure was full to the brim. The farmer also gave him a large wheelbarrow to take the money and the chest away in.

"Good-by!" said Little Claus, and off he went with his money and the big chest with the sexton in it.

There was a wide and deep river on the other side of the wood, the stream was so strong that it was almost impossible to swim against it. A large new bridge had been built across it, and when they got into the very middle of it, Little Claus said quite loud, so that the sexton would hear him—

"What am I to do with this stupid old chest? it might be full of paving stones, it's so heavy! I am quite tired of wheeling it along; I'll just throw it into the river. If it floats down the river to my house, well and good, and if it doesn't, I sha'n't care."

Then he took hold of the chest and raised it up a bit, as if he was about to throw it into the river.

"No, no! let it be!" shouted the sexton. "Let me get out!"

"Hullo!" said Little Claus, pretending to be frightened. "Why, he's still inside it, then I must throw it into the river to drown him."

"Oh no, oh no!" shouted the sexton. "I'll give you a bushel full of money if you'll let me out!"

"Oh, that's another matter," said Little Claus, opening the chest. The sexton crept out at once and pushed the empty chest into the water, and then went home and gave Little Claus a whole bushel of money.

"I got a pretty fair price for that horse I must admit!" said he to himself when he got home to his own room and turned the money out of the wheelbarrow into a heap on the floor. "What a rage Great Claus will be in when he discovers how rich I am become through my one horse, but I won't tell him straight out about it." So he sent a boy to Great Claus to borrow a bushel measure.

"What does he want that for!" thought Great Claus, and he rubbed some tallow on the bottom, so that a little of whatever was to be measured might stick to it. So it did, for when the measure came back three new silver threepenny bits were sticking to it.

"What's this?" said Great Claus, and he ran straight along to Little Claus. "Where on earth did you get all that money?"

"Oh, that was for my horse's hide which I sold last night."

"That was well paid, indeed," said Great

Claus, and he ran home, took an ax and hit all his four horses on the head. He then flayed them and went off to the town with the hides.

"Skins, skins, who will buy skins?" he shouted up and down the streets.

All the shoemakers and tanners in the town came running up and asked him how much he wanted for them.

"A bushel of money for each," said Great Claus.

"Are you mad?" they all said; "do you imagine we have money by the bushel?"

"Skins, skins, who will buy skins?" he shouted again, and the shoemakers took up their measures and the tanners their leather aprons, and beat Great Claus through the town.

"Skins, skins!" they mocked him. "Yes, we'll give you a rawhide. Out of the town with him!" they shouted, and Great Claus had to hurry off as fast as ever he could go. He had never had such a beating in his life.

"Little Claus shall pay for this!" he said when he got home. "I'll kill him for it."

Little Claus' old grandmother had just died in his house; she certainly had been very cross and unkind to him, but now that she was dead, he felt quite sorry about it. He took the dead woman and put her into his warm bed, to see if he could bring her to life again. He meant her to stay there all night, and he would sit on a chair in the corner; he had slept like that before.

As he sat there in the night, the door opened, and in came Great Claus with his ax; he knew where Little Claus' bed stood, and he went straight up to it and hit the dead grandmother a blow on the forehead, thinking that it was Little Claus.

"Just see if you'll cheat me again after that!" he said, and then he went home again.

"What a bad, wicked man he is," said Little Claus; "he was going to kill me there. What a good thing that poor old granny was dead already, or else he would have killed her."

He now dressed his old grandmother in her best Sunday clothes, borrowed a horse of his neighbor, harnessed it to a cart, and set his grandmother on the back seat, so that she could not fall out when the cart moved. Then he started off through the wood. When the sun rose he was just outside a big inn, and Little Claus drew up his horse and went in to get something to eat.

The landlord was a very, very rich man, and a very good man, but he was fiery-tempered, as if he were made of pepper and tobacco.

"Good-morning!" said he to Little Claus;

"you've got your best clothes on very early this morning!"

"Yes," said Little Claus; "I'm going to town with my old grandmother, she's sitting out there in the cart, I can't get her to come in. Won't you take her out a glass of mead? You'll have to shout at her, she's very hard of hearing."

"Yes, she shall have it!" said the innkeeper, and he poured out a large glass of mead which he took out to the dead grandmother in the cart.

"Here is a glass of mead your son has sent!" said the innkeeper, but the dead woman sat quite still and never said a word.

"Don't you hear?" shouted the innkeeper as loud as ever he could; "here is a glass of mead!"

Again he shouted, and then again as loud as ever, but as she did not stir, he got angry and threw the glass of mead in her face, so that the mead ran all over her, and she fell backwards out of the cart, for she was only stuck up and not tied in.

"Now!" shouted Little Claus, as he rushed out of the inn and seized the landlord by the neck, "you have killed my grandmother! Just look, there's a great hole in her forehead!"

"Oh, what a misfortune!" exclaimed the inn-

keeper, clasping his hands; "that's the conse-
quence of my fiery temper! Good Little Claus,
I will give you a bushel of money, and bury
your grandmother as if she had been my own,
if you will only say nothing about it. If you
tell, they will chop my head off, and that is so
nasty."

So Little Claus had a whole bushel of
money, and the innkeeper buried the old
grandmother just as if she had been his own.

When Little Claus got home again with all
his money, he immediately sent over his boy
to Great Claus to borrow his measure.

"What!" said Great Claus, "is he not dead?
I shall have to go and see about it myself!"
So he took the measure over to Little Claus
himself.

"I say, wherever did you get all that
money?" asked he, his eyes round with amazement at what he saw.

"It was my grandmother you killed instead
of me!" said Little Claus. "I have sold her and
got a bushel of money for her!"

"That was good pay, indeed!" said Great
Claus, and he hurried home, took an ax and
killed his old grandmother.

He then put her in a cart and drove off to
the town with her where the apothecary lived,
and asked if he would buy a dead body.

"Who is it, and where did the body come from?" asked the apothecary.

"It is my grandmother, and I have killed her for a bushel of money!" said Great Claus.

"Heaven preserve us!" said the apothecary. "You are talking like a madman; pray don't say such things! You might lose your head!"

And he pointed out to him what a horribly wicked thing he had done, and what a bad man he was. Great Claus was so frightened that he rushed straight out of the shop, jumped into the cart, whipped up his horse and galloped home. The apothecary and everyone else thought he was mad, and so they let him drive off.

"You shall be paid for this!" said Great Claus, when he got out on the highroad. "You shall pay for this, Little Claus!"

As soon as he got home he took the biggest sack he could find, went over to Little Claus and said:

"You have deceived me again! First I killed my horses, and then my old grandmother! It's all your fault, but you sha'n't have the chance of cheating me again!"

Then he took Little Claus by the waist and put him into the sack, put it on his back, and shouted to him:

"I'm going to drown you now!"

It was a long way to go before he came to the river, and Little Claus was not so light to carry. The road passed close by the church in which the organ was playing, and the people were singing beautifully. Great Claus put down the sack with Little Claus in it close by the church door, and thought he would like to go in and hear a psalm before he went any further. Little Claus could not get out of the bag, and all the people were in church, so he went in, too.

"Oh dear, oh dear!" sighed Little Claus in the sack. He turned and twisted, but it was impossible to undo the cord. Just then an old cattle drover with white hair and a tall stick in his hand came along. He had a whole drove of cows and bulls before him. They ran against the sack Little Claus was in, and upset it.

"Oh dear!" sighed Little Claus; "I am so young to be going to the Kingdom of Heaven!"

"And I," said the cattle drover, "am so old and cannot get there yet!"

"Open the sack!" shouted Little Claus. "Get in in place of me, and you will get to heaven directly!"

"That will just suit me," said the cattle drover, undoing the sack for Little Claus, who immediately sprang out. "You must look after

"You must look after the cattle now," said the old
man as he crept into the sack.

the cattle now," said the old man as he crept into the sack. Little Claus tied it up and walked off, driving the cattle before him.

A little while after Great Claus came out of the church. He took up the sack on his back, and certainly thought it had grown lighter, for the old cattle drover was not more than half the weight of Little Claus. "How light he seems to have got; that must be because I have been to church and said my prayers!" Then he went on to the river, which was both wide and deep, and threw the sack with the old cattle drover in it into the water, shouting as he did so (for he thought it was Little Claus), "Now, you won't cheat me again!" Then he went homewards, but when he reached the crossroads he met Little Claus with his herd of cattle.

"What's the meaning of this?" exclaimed Great Claus. "Didn't I drown you?"

"Yes," said Little Claus, "it's only about half an hour since you threw me into the river!"

"But where did you get all those splendid beasts?" asked Great Claus.

"They are sea-cattle," said Little Claus. "I will tell you the whole story, and indeed I thank you heartily for drowning me. I'm at the top of the tree now and a very rich man, I can tell you. I was so frightened when I was in the sack! The wind whistled in my ears when you threw me over the bridge into the cold water. I immediately sank to the bottom, but I was not hurt, for the grass is beautifully soft down there. The sack was opened at once by a beautiful maiden in snow-white clothes with a green wreath on her wet hair. She took my hand and said, 'Are you there, Little Claus? Here are some cattle for you, and a mile further up the road you will come upon another herd, which I will give you, too!' Then I saw that the river was a great highway for the sea-folk. Down at the bottom of it they walked and drove about, from the sea right up to the end of the river. The flowers were lovely and the grass was so fresh; the fishes which swam about glided close to me just like birds in the air. How nice the people were, and what a lot of cattle strolling about in the ditches."

"But why did you come straight up here again then?" asked Great Claus. "I shouldn't have done that, if it was so fine down there."

"Oh," said Little Claus, "that's because I'm wise. You remember I told you that the mermaid said that a mile further up the road— and by the road she means the river, for she can't go anywhere else—I should find another herd of cattle waiting for me. Well, I know how many bends there are in the river, and

what a roundabout way it would be. It's ever
so much shorter if you can come up on dry
land and take the short cuts, you save a cou-
ple of miles by it, and get the cattle much
sooner."

"Oh, you are a fortunate man!" said Great
Claus. "Do you think I could get some sea-
cattle if I were to go down to the bottom of
the river?"

"I'm sure you would," said Little Claus; "but
I can't carry you in the sack to the river;
you're too heavy for me. If you like to walk
there and then get into the sack, I'll throw you
into the river with the greatest pleasure in
the world."

"Thank you," said Great Claus; "but if I
don't get any sea-cattle when I get down
there, see if I don't give you a sound
thrashing."

"Oh! don't be so hard on me." They then
walked off to the river. As soon as the cattle
saw the water, they rushed down to drink.
"See what a hurry they're in," said Little
Claus; "they want to get down to the bottom
again."

"Now, help me," said Great Claus. He then
crept into a big sack which had been lying
across the back of one of the cows. "Put a big

stone in, or I'm afraid I sha'n't sink," said
Great Claus.

"Oh, that'll be all right," said Little Claus,
but he put a big stone into the sack and gave
it a push. Plump went the sack and Great
Claus was in the river, where he sank to the
bottom at once.

"I'm afraid he won't find any cattle," said
Little Claus, as he drove his herd home.

The Swineherd

THERE WAS ONCE a poor prince; he had only a tiny kingdom, but it was big enough to allow him to marry, and he was bent upon marrying.

Now it certainly was rather bold of him to say to the emperor's daughter, "Will you have me?" He did, however, venture to say so, for his name was known far and wide, and there were hundreds of princesses who would have said, "Yes," and "Thank you, kindly," but see if she would!

Just let us hear about it.

A rose tree grew on the grave of the prince's father, it was such a beautiful rose tree; it only bloomed every fifth year, and then only bore one blossom, but what a rose that was! By merely smelling it, one forgot all one's cares and sorrows.

Then he had a nightingale which sang as if

every lovely melody in the world dwelt in her little throat. This rose and this nightingale were to be given to the princess, so they were put into great silver caskets and sent to her.

The emperor had them carried before him into the great hall where the princess was playing at "visiting" with her ladies-in-waiting; they had nothing else to do. When she saw the caskets with the gifts she clapped her hands with delight!

"If it were only a little pussy-cat!" said she,—but there was the lovely rose.

"Oh, how exquisitely it is made!" said all the ladies-in-waiting.

"It is more than beautiful," said the emperor; "it is neat."

But the princess touched it, and then she was ready to cry.

"Fie, papa!" she said. "It is not made, it is a real one!"

"Fie," said all the ladies-in-waiting. "It is a real one!"

"Well, let us see what there is in the other casket, before we get angry," said the Emperor, and out came the nightingale. It sang so beautifully that at first no one could find anything to say against it.

"*Superbe! charmant!*" said the ladies-in-waiting, for they all had a smattering of French, one spoke it worse than the other.

"How that bird reminds me of our lamented empress's musical box," said an old courtier. "Ah, yes, they are the same tunes, and the same beautiful execution."

"So they are," said the emperor, and he cried like a little child.

"I should hardly think it could be a real one," said the princess.

"Yes, it is a real one," said those who had brought it.

"Oh, let that bird fly away then," said the princess, and she would not hear of allowing the prince to come. But he was not to be crushed. He stained his face brown and black, and, pressing his cap over his eyes, he knocked at the door.

"Good-morning, Emperor," said he. "Can I be taken into service in the palace?"

"Well, there are so many wishing to do that," said the emperor, "but let me see!—yes, I need somebody to look after the pigs, for we have so many of them."

So the prince was made imperial swineherd. A horrid little room was given him near the pigsties, and here he had to live. He sat busily at work all day, and by the evening he had made a beautiful little cooking pot; it had bells all around it and when the pot boiled they tinkled delightfully and played the old tune:

> "Ach du lieber Augustin,
>   Alles ist weg, weg, weg!"*

But the greatest charm of all about it was, that, by holding one's finger in the steam, one could immediately smell all the dinners that were being cooked at every stove in the town. Now this was a very different matter from a rose.

The princess came walking along with all her ladies-in-waiting, and when she heard the tune she stopped and looked pleased, for she could play "du lieber Augustin" herself; it was her only tune, and she could only play it with one finger.

"Why, that is my tune," she said. "This must be a cultivated swineherd. Go and ask him what the instrument costs."

So one of the ladies-in-waiting had to go into his room, but she put pattens on first.

"How much do you want for the pot?" she asked.

---

*Alas, dear Augustin,
  All is lost, lost, lost!

"I must have ten kisses from the princess," said the swineherd.

"Heaven preserve us!" said the lady.

"I won't take less," said the swineherd.

"Well, what does he say?" asked the princess.

"I really cannot tell you," said the lady-in-waiting, "it is so shocking."

"Then you must whisper it." And she whispered it.

"He is a wretch!" said the princess, and went away at once. But she had only gone a little way when she heard the bells tinkling beautifully:

"Ach du lieber Augustin."

"Go and ask him if he will take ten kisses from the ladies-in-waiting."

"No, thank you," said the swineherd—"ten kisses from the princess, or I keep my pot."

"How tiresome it is," said the princess. "Then you will have to stand round me, so that no one may see."

So the ladies-in-waiting stood round her and spread out their skirts while the swineherd took his ten kisses, and then the pot was hers.

What a delight it was to them. The pot was

So the ladies-in-waiting stood round her and
spread out their skirts.

kept on the boil day and night. They knew what was cooking on every stove in the town, from the chamberlain's to the shoemaker's. The ladies-in-waiting danced about and clapped their hands.

"We know who has sweet soup and pancakes for dinner, and who has cutlets! How amusing it is."

"Highly interesting," said the mistress of the robes.

"One must encourage art," she said. "I am the emperor's daughter."

"Heaven preserve us!" they all said.

The swineherd—that is to say, the prince, only nobody knew that he was not a real swineherd—did not let the day pass in idleness, and he now constructed a rattle. When it was swung round it played all the waltzes, galops and jig tunes which have ever been heard since the creation of the world.

"But this is *superbe!*" said the princess, as she walked by. "I have never heard finer compositions. Go and ask him what the instrument costs, but let us have no more kissing."

"He wants a hundred kisses from the princess!" said the lady-in-waiting.

"I think he is mad!" said the princess, and she went away, but she had not gone far when she stopped.

"One must encourage art," she said. "I am

the emperor's daughter. Tell him he can have ten kisses, the same as yesterday, and he can take the others from the ladies-in-waiting."

"But we don't like that at all," said the ladies.

"Oh, nonsense! If I can kiss him you can do the same. Remember that I pay you wages as well as give you board and lodging." So the lady-in-waiting had to go again.

"A hundred kisses from the princess, or let each keep his own."

"Stand in front of me," said she, and all the ladies stood around, while he kissed her.

"Whatever is the meaning of that crowd round the pigsties?" said the emperor, as he stepped out on to the veranda; he rubbed his eyes and put on his spectacles. "Why, it is the ladies-in-waiting, what game are they up to? I must go and see!" So he pulled up the heels of his slippers, for they were shoes which he had trodden down.

Bless us, what a hurry he was in! When he got into the yard, he walked very softly and the ladies were so busy counting the kisses, so that there should be fair play, and neither too few, nor too many kisses, that they never heard the emperor. He stood on tiptoe.

"What is all this?" he said when he saw what was going on, and he hit them on the head with his slipper just as the swineherd was taking his eighty-sixth kiss.

"Out you go!" said the emperor, for he was furious, and both the princess and the prince were put out of his realm.

There she stood crying, and the swineherd scolded, and the rain poured down in torrents.

"Oh, miserable creature that I am! If only I had accepted the handsome prince. Oh, how unhappy I am!"

The swineherd went behind a tree, wiped the black and brown stain from his face, and threw away his ugly clothes. When he stepped out dressed as a prince, he was so handsome that the princess could not help curtseying to him.

"I am come to despise thee," he said. "Thou wouldst not have an honorable prince, thou couldst not prize the rose, or the nightingale, but thou wouldst kiss the swineherd for a trumpery musical box! As thou hast made thy bed, so must thou lie upon it!"

Then he went back into his own little kingdom and shut and locked the door. So she had to stand outside and sing in earnest—

"Ach du lieber Augustin,
Alles ist weg, weg, weg!"